CHICAGO PUBLIC LIBRARY

for me
for you
for later

FIRST STEPS TO SPENDING, SHARING, AND SAVING™

City of Chicago
Mayor Rahm Emanuel

Chicago
Public
Library

chicagopubliclibrary.org

Chicago Public Library Foundation

PNC Grow Up Great®

characters created by lauren child

But I've Used ALL of MY Pocket Change

dial books for young readers
an imprint of Penguin Group (USA) Inc.

Text based on

the script written by

Carol Noble

Illustrations from

the TV animation

produced by Tiger Aspect

DIAL BOOKS FOR YOUNG READERS
A division of Penguin Young Readers Group
Published by The Penguin Group
Penguin Group (USA) Inc., 375 Hudson Street, New York, NY 10014, U.S.A.
Penguin Group (Canada), 90 Eglinton Avenue East, Suite 700, Toronto, Ontario, Canada M4P 2Y3 (a division of Pearson Penguin Canada Inc.)
Penguin Books Ltd, 80 Strand, London WC2R 0RL, England
Penguin Ireland, 25 St. Stephen's Green, Dublin 2, Ireland (a division of Penguin Books Ltd)
Penguin Group (Australia), 250 Camberwell Road, Camberwell, Victoria 3124, Australia (a division of Pearson Australia Group Pty Ltd)
Penguin Books India Pvt Ltd, 11 Community Centre, Panchsheel Park, New Delhi - 110 017, India
Penguin Group (NZ), 67 Apollo Drive, Rosedale, Auckland 0632, New Zealand (a division of Pearson New Zealand Ltd)
Penguin Books (South Africa) (Pty) Ltd, 24 Sturdee Avenue, Rosebank, Johannesburg 2196, South Africa
Penguin Books Ltd, Registered Offices: 80 Strand, London WC2R 0RL, England

I have this little sister Lola.
She is small and very funny.
Today Lola is really excited because
Granny and Grandpa are taking us both to the zoo.
"I can't wait to see the seals, Charlie. Bark! Bark!"

When we are getting ready, Lola says,
"What are you going to buy from the zoo shop, Charlie?

"I'm getting a completely good
seal toy for the bath.
Just like Lotta's!"

And I say,
"I'd really like one of those
books that shows where
all the animals
come from."

Then I say,
"Lola, you can't eat
your **tangerine** now.
Mum packed it for lunch.
You're not very good
at **saving** things for later."

"Yes I am, Charlie."

And I say,
"You are **not!**

"When you read a
book, you NEVER
                    wait for the end.
You always skip ahead!"

"Oh no!
Now I know
what **happens**."

In the car on the way to the zoo, I say,
    "Maybe you shouldn't eat your sandwich now, Lola.
You should save it for later."

But Lola just says,
    "Charlie, what is this box?"

"It's a camera. Dad bought some for
    us so we can take pictures of
all the animals at the zoo."

"Oooh, look at
that, Charlie."

Click!

Click!

Click!

I say,
"Lola, the camera is not
just for clicking—
it's for taking photographs."

And Lola says,
"Oh. Okay, Charlie."

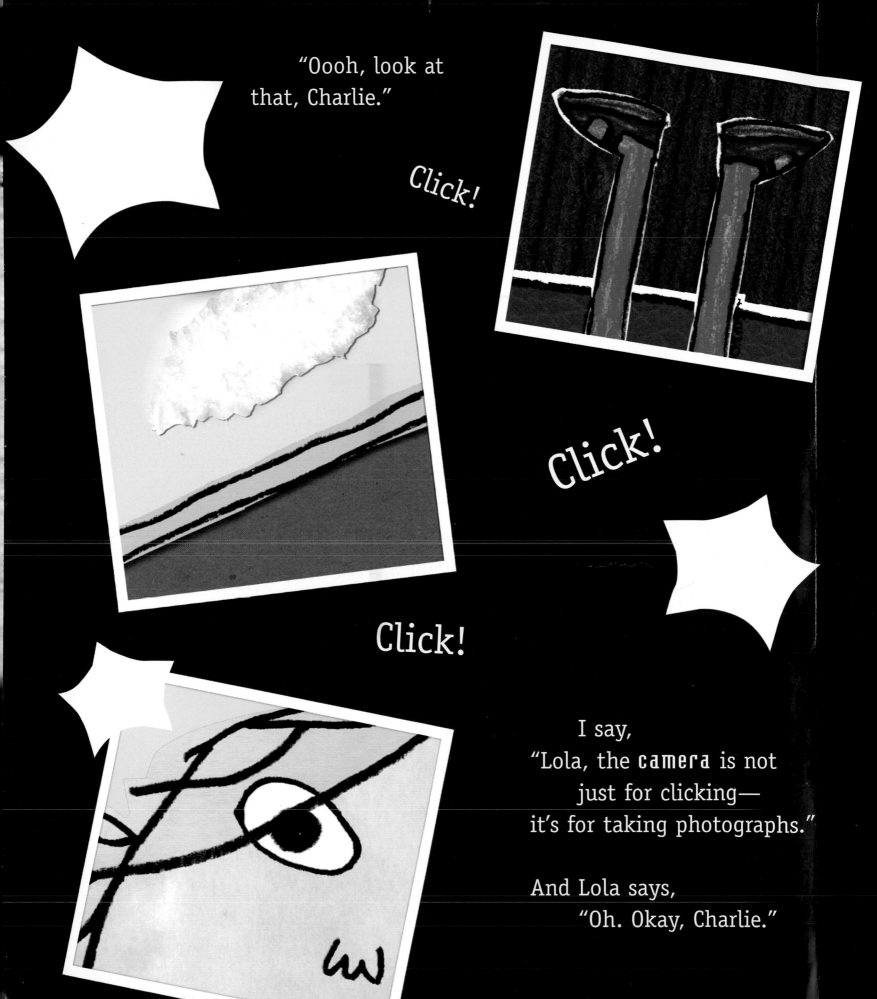

Granny and Grandpa stop at the park so
Lola and I can feed the **ducks**.

I break off little pieces of bread,

but Lola throws all
of hers straight
into the pond.

Lola says,
"I've run out of bread, Charlie.
Please may I have
some of **yours**?"

I say,
"All right, Lola."

When we get to the **zoo**, Granny and
Grandpa say we can look
at any animal we want.

I say,
"Lola! Look at the **giraffes**!"

"Ooh, they're especially good," says Lola. "But my clicky **camera** is completely filled up, Charlie. **Please** can I borrow **yours**?"

Click!

Click!

And I say, "Okay, Lola. But just take one photo because I really want to photograph the **anteaters** and the **armadillos**."

Click!

Then Lola says,
"I'm going to
ask Granny if I can
buy a **zoo** balloon!"

And I say,
"Don't you think you should
save your **pocket money**
if you want to buy your
seal toy at the **zoo** shop later?"

"But I've got lots of money, Charlie," says Lola.

At lunchtime, Lola says,
"Charlie, please can I have some of your sandwich?"

"But Lola . . . you've already had yours."

"Please, Charlie."

I say,
"You can have a little bit."

Lola says,
   "I am going to buy
some pink milk because I
   really am extremely thirsty."

I say,
   "Lola, you won't have
anything left to spend in the
   zoo shop."

"Oh yes I will, Charlie.
   I still have
one more bit of money."

When we get to the **seal** tank,
Lola says, "Oooh. Bark! Bark!
Can I **please** borrow your **camera**, Charlie?
I absolutely must take a
photograph of the **seals**."

At the **zoo** shop, Lola says,
"Now I must go and find my **seal** toy."

And I say,
"Look, Lola. This is The Complete Animal Atlas.
It has all the animals
and where they come from . . .

"There's an elephant,

an armadillo,

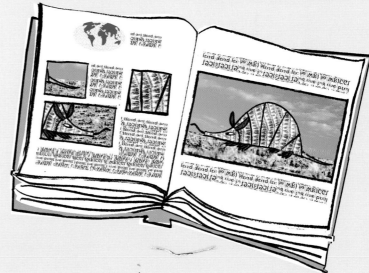

and a bald eagle!"

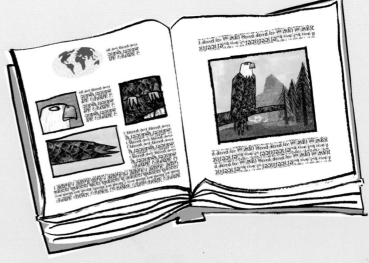

But Lola isn't listening.
Instead she says,
"The man said I didn't have enough
money for my seal toy."

I say,
"That's because you spent
your pocket money on all
those other things."

Lola says,
"But what will I do now, Charlie?
Now I won't have a toy like Lotta's."

So I say,
"Here you are, Lola.
You can have some
of MY money."

And Lola says,
"Oh, thank you
ever so
much,
Charlie."

On the way home, Lola says,
    "Are there any seals in your animal book, Charlie?"

And I say,
    "I didn't buy the
        book because I didn't
    have enough money."

Lola says,
"I thought you had lots
of **money** because you
saved it up."

"No, Lola," I say.
"I didn't have enough
for my **book** after
I gave you the
money for the
seal toy."

The next day Lola starts
to save things up.

Whenever we get
pocket money,
Lola puts hers
straight into
her **piggy bank**.

And she doesn't skip
to the end of her
book anymore.

"I'll save
this for later.

And one of these.

And this."

When we go to the **duck** pond, Lola only uses
a little bit of her bread.
And she even gives some to me.

I say,

"Thanks, Lola. I've nearly saved up
enough **pocket money** to buy an
animal **atlas**. When Dad takes
us to the **bookshop**, I'm definitely
going to buy it."

And Lola says,
"I've been saving up too,
Charlie. I might buy a
book about seals.
Bark! Bark!"

At the **bookshop**, I say,
"Oh no. This costs more than the
book in the **zoo** shop.
I haven't got enough **money**!"

"Don't worry, Charlie," says Lola.
"You can have some of MY pocket money
because I've saved lots."

"Thank you, Lola,"
I say.

Then I say, "Ugh, what's that in your pocket, Lola?"

"It's my tangerine, Charlie.
I've been saving it up
        just in case we need a snack!"